BEETHOVEN

SONATA NO. 21 IN C MAJOR
OPUS 53
FOR THE PIANO

(Grande Sonate)

EDITED BY STEWART GORDON

AN ALFRED MASTERWORK EDITION

Cover art: Ludwig van Beethoven *(1770–1827)*
by Karl Stieler (1781–1858)
Oil on canvas, 1819
Beethoven-Haus, Bonn, Germany
Erich Lessing/Art Resource, NY
Additional art: © *Planet Art*

LUDWIG VAN BEETHOVEN
Sonata No. 21 in C Major ("Waldstein"), Op. 53
(Grande Sonate)

Edited by Stewart Gordon

Foreword

About This Edition

Ludwig van Beethoven (1770–1827) is often regarded as a link between the balance and clarity of Classicism and the emotional intensity and freedom of Romanticism. In his 32 piano sonatas, he experimented constantly with structure and content. These works span a period of almost 30 years of Beethoven's mature creative life. He used the sonatas as a workshop in which to try out innovations, many of his compositional techniques appearing in the sonatas first and then later in chamber or symphonic works.

Beethoven completed the Op. 53 between May and November of 1803. Sketches of the Op. 53 show that the composer was working on the sonata along with the Symphony No. 3, Op. 55 ("Eroica"), and the opera *Fidelio*, Op. 70, especially the overture to it known as *Leonore Overture No. 2*. Sketches for the Op. 53 are particularly interesting for studying the process through which the composer transformed initial thematic fragments into final versions.

Count Ferdinand Ernest Gabriel von Waldstein (1762–1823) had been a patron of Beethoven from the time both of them resided in Bonn, the Count having been dispatched there from Vienna on a diplomatic mission. It was probably through the influence of the Count that the Elector of Bonn, Maximilian Franz (1756–1801), sponsored Beethoven to go to Vienna to study with Haydn. At the time of Beethoven's departure for Vienna, Waldstein wrote in the composer's autograph book, *"May you receive the spirit of Mozart through the hands of Haydn."*

An autograph for the Op. 53 is extant, but there is speculation as to whether or not it was the basis used for the first edition, due to the number of differences between the two sources. Perhaps the engraver's carelessness can account for the differences; on the other hand, scholars have speculated that if, indeed, the engraver of the first edition was working from another manuscript, it may have represented the composer's final editing of the sonata.

Thus, the primary sources for this edition are both the autograph manuscript and the first edition published in Vienna, Austria, by Bureau d'Arts et d'Industrie in 1805. Additionally, a number of other esteemed editions were referenced (see "Sources Consulted for This Edition" on page 3) when decisions have had to be made due to lack of clarity or inconsistency in the early sources, or when realization of ornamentation was open to question.

Recommended solutions to problems are suggested in footnotes in this edition. If, however, a problem is such that it is open to several solutions, other editors' conclusions are also often included. In this way students and their teachers are not only offered choices in individual cases but, more importantly, gain an awareness of the editorial and performance problems that attend studying and playing this music.

The insurmountable problems that arise in trying to distinguish between the staccato dot and the wedge in these works have led this editor to join ranks with most others in using but one marking (dot) for both symbols.

Like almost all other editors, I have chosen not to indicate pedaling markings in the sonatas except those left by the composer. The matter of pedaling, especially as might be applicable to music of this era, must be based on innumerable choices that result from stylistic awareness and careful listening, these possibilities changing as different instruments or performance venues are encountered.

Both autographs and first editions contain inconsistencies. First editions especially are prone to many discrepancies, such as differences in articulation in parallel passages in expositions and recapitulations of movements in sonata-allegro form, or the many cases of an isolated note in passagework without the articulation shown for all its neighbors. Even those editors whose philosophy is to be as faithful to the composer as possible subscribe to the practice of correcting these small discrepancies without taking note of such through the addition of parentheses. This edition also subscribes to that practice to avoid cluttering the performer's pages with what would turn out to be a myriad of parenthetical changes. By the same token, this editor has proceeded with an attitude of caution and inquiry, so that such changes have been made only in the most obvious cases of error or omission. If, in the opinion of the editor, there seemed to be the slightest chance that such inconsistencies could represent conscious variation or musical intent on the part of the composer, the issue has been highlighted, either by the use of parentheses that show editorial additions or footnotes that outline discrepancies and discuss possible musical intent on the part of the composer.

Fingering in parentheses indicates alternative fingering. When a single fingering number attends a chord or two vertical notes, the number indicates the uppermost or lowermost note. Octaves on black keys are usually fingered 1-4, but it is acknowledged that such fingering may prove too much of a stretch for some hands. Thus, (4) in parenthesis indicates that players with small hands may want to substitute 1-5.

Ornaments such as trills, turns, and mordents are discussed in footnotes. When a single rapid appoggiatura or grace note is not footnoted, the performer should choose whether to execute it before the beat or on the beat. However, in some cases this editor indicates a preference for on-the-beat execution in the music by using a dotted line that connects the ornamental note with the base note with which it is to be played.

Sources Consulted for This Edition

Beethoven, Ludwig van. *Sonatas for Piano.* Edited by Eugen d'Albert. New York: Carl Fischer, 1981; originally published in 1902.

Beethoven, Ludwig van. *Sonaten für Klavier zu zwei Händen.* Edited by Claudio Arrau, revised by Lothar Hoffmann-Erbrecht. Frankfurt: C. F. Peters, 1973.

Beethoven, Ludwig van. *Sonatas for the Piano.* Edited by Hans von Bülow and Sigmund Lebert, translated by Theodore Baker. New York: G. Schirmer, 1894; currently distributed by Hal Leonard, Milwaukee.

Beethoven, Ludwig van. *Sonatas for Piano.* Edited by Alfredo Casella. Rome: G. Ricordi, 1919.

Beethoven, Ludwig van. *Complete Pianoforte Sonatas.* Edited by Harold Craxton, annotated Donald Francis Tovey. London: Associated Board of the Royal School of Music, 1931.

Beethoven, Ludwig van. *Sonaten für Klavier.* Edited by Peter Hauschild. Vienna and Mainz: Wiener Urtext Edition, Schott/Universal, 1999.

Beethoven, Ludwig van. *Sonaten für Klavier.* Edited by Louis Köhler and Adolf Ruthardt. Frankfurt: C. F. Peters; originally published in 1890.

Beethoven, Ludwig van. *Sonatas for Piano.* Edited by Carl Krebs. Los Angeles: Alfred Publishing; Kalmus Editions, originally published in 1898.

Beethoven, Ludwig van. *Sonaten für Klavier zu zwei Händen.* Edited by Carl Adolf Martienssen. New York: C. F. Peters, 1948.

Beethoven, Ludwig van. *Complete Piano Sonatas.* Edited by Heinrich Schenker with a new introduction by Carl Schachter. New York: Dover, 1975; originally published in 1934.

Beethoven, Ludwig van. *Sonatas for the Pianoforte.* Edited by Artur Schnabel. New York: Simon & Schuster, 1935.

Beethoven, Ludwig van. *Piano Sonatas.* Edited by Kendall Taylor. Melbourne: Allans Publishing PTY. Limited, 1989. Currently distributed by Elkin Music International, Inc. Pompano Beach, Florida.

Beethoven, Ludwig van. *Klaviersonaten.* Edited by B. A. Wallner, fingering by Conrad Hansen. Munich: G. Henle, 1952, 1980.

For Further Reading

The Letters of Beethoven; 3 vols. Edited and translated by Emily Anderson. London: St. Martin's Press, 1961.

Bach, Carl Philipp Emanuel. *Essay on the True Art of Playing Keyboard Instruments.* Translated and edited by William J. Mitchell. New York: W. W. Norton, 1949.

Czerny, Carl. *On the Proper Performance of All Beethoven's Works for the Piano.* Edited by Paul Badura-Skoda. Vienna: Universal Edition, 1970.

Dannreuther, Edward. *Musical Ornamentation.* 2 volumes. London: Novello & Co., 1893–95.

Hummel, Johann Nepomuk. *A Complete Theoretical and Practical Course of Instructions on the Art of Playing the Piano Forte, Commencing with the Simplest Elementary Principles and Including Every Information Requisite to the Most Finished Style of Performance.* London: T. Boosey & Co., 1829.

Kullak, Franz. *Beethoven's Piano Playing, with an Essay on the Execution of the Trill.* Translated by Theodore Baker. New York: G. Schirmer, 1901.

Newman, William S. *Beethoven on Beethoven: Playing His Piano Music His Way.* New York: W. W. Norton, 1988.

Newman, William S. *Performance Practices in Beethoven's Piano Sonatas.* New York: W. W. Norton, 1971.

Dedicated to the Count Ferdinand von Waldstein

Sonata No. 21 in C Major
(Grande Sonate)

Ludwig van Beethoven (1770–1827)
Op. 53

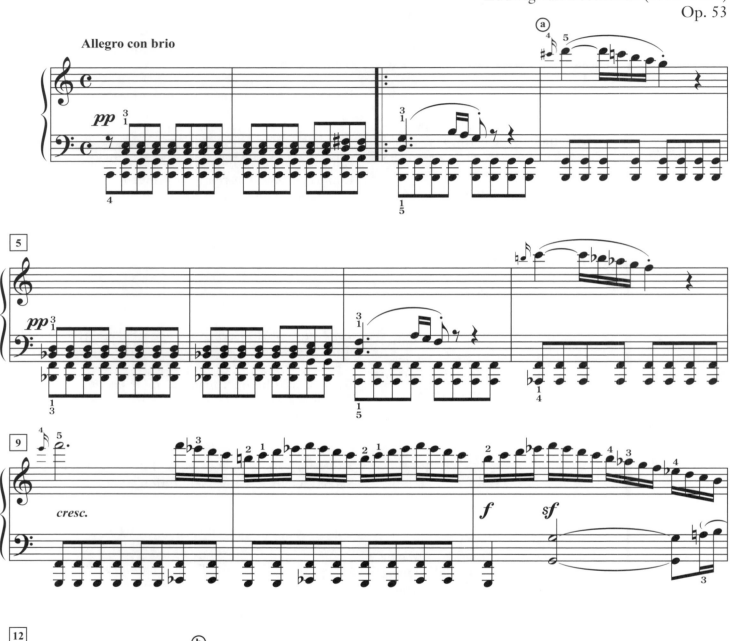

ⓐ Both the autograph and the first edition show all grace notes in this movement as small sixteenth notes (♪).
Of the referenced editors, Arrau, Hauschild, Krebs, Schenker, Taylor, and Wallner keep the original notation.
D'Albert, Bülow, Casella, Köhler, Martienssen, Schnabel, and Tovey show ♪ instead. Taylor recommends
playing the notes on the beat, rapidly, but not as crushed notes (*acciaccatura*).

ⓑ Bülow suggests the fermata should equal an extra whole note, counted in time. Casella objects to the "squareness" of this
recommendation, suggesting instead an extra dotted half note (♩.) or whole note tied to a quarter (𝅝 ♩).

ⓒ The autograph shows two decresc. indications in both measures 31 and 194, one for the entrance of each hand. The first edition shows two indications in measure 31, but only one in 194. Of the referenced editors, d'Albert, Köhler, Krebs, Martienssen, and Schenker follow the first edition, repeating the inconsistency. Only Schnabel and Taylor preserve both indications in both places, Taylor pointing to the conceptual importance of having both in a footnote.

(d) The autograph and the first edition show cresc. in measure 70, but editorial agreement deems this an error, favoring instead the decresc. indicated in both sources in the parallel passage at measure 233.

(e) Six of the referenced editors and this editor show fingering that suggests starting the trill on the main note. This execution is possible by using sixteenth notes for the trill in coordination with the RH sixteenth notes, with a sixteenth-note triplet at the end to accommodate the after-notes (*nachschlag*). Only Bülow suggests starting on the upper accessory. In Bülow's realization, the ease of executing the after-notes is offset by an intervallic pattern that weakens the dominant sonority, so this editor does not recommend it.

ⓕ In his edition, Czerny shows the LH of measure 106, beats 3 and 4, as F, A-flat, D-flat, F. Casella speculates Beethoven made this change after the first edition had gone to press. Bülow argues against the change in a footnote. The autograph shows F, B-flat, D-flat, F.

ⓖ The autograph shows the first two beats of measure 107 as F-flat, G-flat, B-flat, and D-flat. The flat is missing from the F in the first edition. All of the referenced editors except Taylor follow the first edition, Hauschild and Wallner noting the discrepancy in a footnote. Following the first edition rather than the autograph ties in with the theory that another autograph copy was used as the basis for the first edition's engraving and/or that the composer continued to revise his work at each stage of the publication process (see the introductory notes to this sonata). Taylor states that the case for the F-flat is strengthened by the fact that using it would render measure 107 harmonically parallel to measures 109 and 111. Such an argument, however, does not take into account the use of C-natural in the LH figuration of measure 110, where Beethoven could have used C-flat if he had wanted parallel harmonic progressions.

(h) The autograph shows the following RH at the opening of measure 233.

The composer then uses repeat symbols (⅏) for the rest of that measure and measure 234. The engraver of the first edition reproduces this figure with yet another alteration, substituting B for G at the second sixteenth note. Most of the referenced editors simply present these measures with figuration parallel to that in measures 70–71. Schenker, Schnabel, Wallner, and Taylor point to these irregularities, Taylor even deeming the figuration in the autograph "attractive."

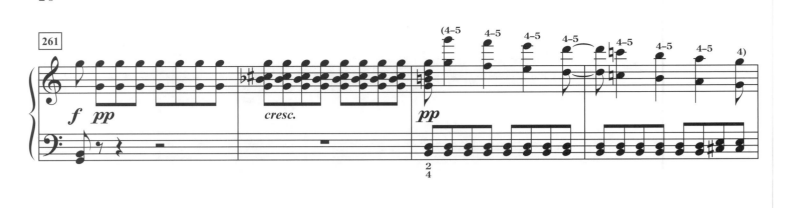

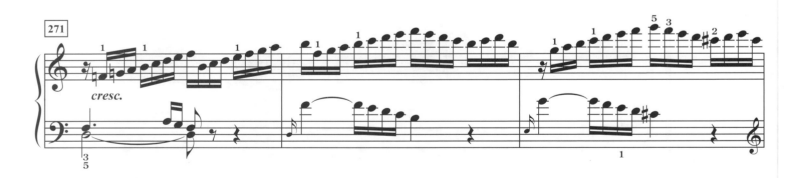

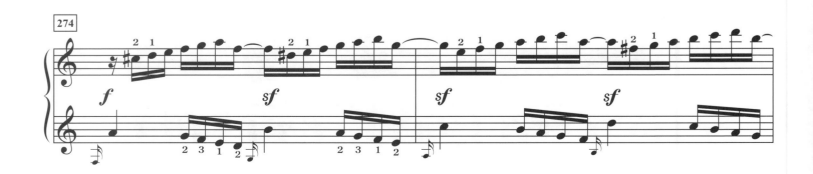

The grace notes on the downbeats of measures 10 and 12 are written as small thirty-second notes in both the autograph and the first edition. Arrau, Hauschild, Schenker, Wallner, and Taylor preserve this notation. (Krebs may have attempted to do so, but managed only sixteenth notes.) The remaining referenced editors use small eighth notes with a slash through the stem (♪). Taylor and Tovey make a case for playing the grace notes on the beat, notwithstanding the fact that the LH doubling in measure 10 might suggest rapid execution before the beat.

Attacca subito il Rondo

ⓑ The two B-flats in the LH starting on beat 4 are not tied in either the autograph or the first edition. D'Albert, Bülow, Casella, Köhler, and Tovey add ties. Schnabel and Taylor write footnotes urging repetition of the B-flat.

ⓒ The grace note on beat 6 in measure 14 is written as a small sixteenth note in both the autograph (where it is barely visible) and the first edition. Arrau, Hauschild, Krebs, Schenker, Wallner, and Taylor preserve this notation. The remainder of the referenced editors substitutes a small eighth note with a slash through the stem (♪).

(a) The autograph shows only *allegretto*. The *moderato* appears in the first edition.

(b) The pedaling throughout this movement comes from both the autograph and the first edition. Beethoven's interest in pedal effects has been evidenced before in the piano sonatas. That Beethoven wanted a coloristic sonority with some degree of blurring seems certain. However, achieving whatever effect the composer wanted on today's instruments that are more resonant is problematic for many. Of the referenced editors, Köhler and Bülow change the original pedaling to achieve harmonic clarity. Schenker, Taylor, and Tovey write notes suggesting unspecified patterns of "half-pedaling" (i.e., half-damping), Taylor and Tovey indicating that using the sostenuto (middle) pedal when it is available might be helpful. Casella and Schnabel in notes extol the originality of the composer's sonic conception and insist that the performer follow the original pedaling. The remaining editors simply reproduce the original pedaling without comment. This editors sides with those who attempt to follow Beethoven's markings exactly, which is possible on most pianos with careful attention to touch, balance, and exact pedal releases.

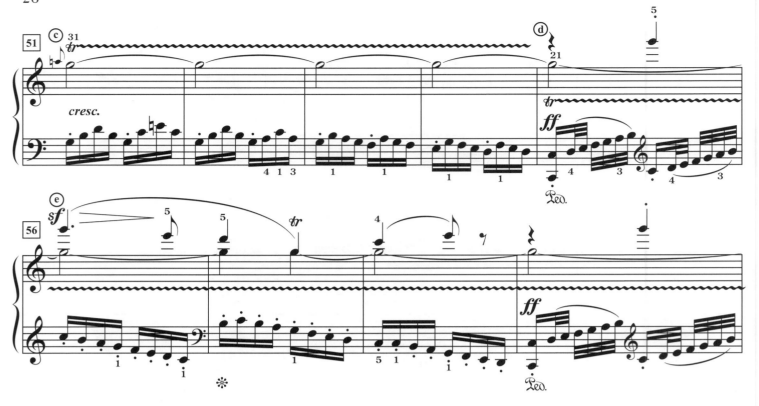

(c) The RH grace note raises questions that have far-reaching effects in this movement. Did the composer write the grace note to ensure starting on the upper accessory in an age when doing so was changing? Or is the grace note meant to be played rapidly before the downbeat to ensure starting the downbeat with the main note? If the performer uses a measured trill (sextuplets are often suggested), then downbeats of ensuing measures will begin with whichever note was used to start the trill (see footnote (d)).

(d) At the end of the autograph Beethoven wrote out two possible realizations of measure 285 (see footnote (l)). Some editors have used these composer's examples as the basis for approaching all the passages in this movement where one hand is required to both trill and play the main theme (e.g., measures 55–61, 168–174, 337–343, and 485–506). This approach raises problems: the frequent stretch of the interval of a seventh at the onset of the melody (e.g., see beat 2 of measure 55), and the fact that at one point a G in the melody forms the interval of a major second with the trill (e.g., see beat 2 of measure 57). Arrau, Hauschild, Köhler, and Wallner do not address this issue. Instead, they suggest fingering that is in keeping with starting beats with the upper note, except for places where the aforementioned interval of a second would occur. In those spots, the starting note shifts so that it coincides with the melodic G. Schenker, Schnabel, Tovey, and Taylor provide notes that suggest strict adherence to Beethoven's model, although Taylor allows the so-called "false trill" as a possibility. Bülow simply rewrites the passages using the "false trill," a technique that J. S. Bach had exploited in Variation 28 of the "Goldberg" Variations (S. 988) and both Czerny and Hummel had illustrated in piano methods.

D'Albert, Casella, Martienssen, and this editor allow for shifting the trill so that the melodic notes occur with the main note of the trill. William S. Newman agrees with allowing the execution of these passages to follow patterns that are more pianistic, suggesting that Beethoven may have lost touch with the physical aspect of playing the piano due to his increasing deafness. (*Beethoven on Beethoven: Playing His Piano Music His Way*; W. W. Norton, New York, 1988, p. 216.) This editor uses the following arrangement:

(e) The autograph shows *sf* on the downbeats of measures 56, 169, 173, 338, and 342. (This mark is missing from measure 60, probably an oversight.) The first edition shows none of these sforzandi. Krebs, Schenker, and Schnabel follow the first edition. All of the other referenced editors either point out this discrepancy in a footnote or add the sforzandi into the text. A second issue is that the first edition shows no slurring in measures 60–61, 173–174, or 341–342. Slurring is missing in measures 60–61 of the autograph as well. Most editors, including this one, believe these parallel passages should be consistent and add slurs accordingly. Only Krebs and Schenker demur, following instead the first edition.

28

(f) Measures 101, 105, 113 as well as a later group, 395, 397, and 399, employ multiple eighth and quarter rests in lieu of whole rests. As this notation exists in both the autograph and the first edition, it is believed that the composer used the device to show exactly where to release the damper pedal. Seven of the referenced editors adopt this multi-rest notation, with Schenker, Schnabel, Taylor, and Wallner pointing out the exactness in notating the pedal releases in footnotes. Krebs and Tovey use less exact notation, the latter suggesting unclearly some kind of pedal adjustment in measures 100 and 104 to alleviate the harmonic blur. D'Albert, Bülow, Casella, and Köhler inexcusably alter the composer's pedaling to ensure harmonic clarity.

(g) The pedaling for measures 235 through the downbeat of measure 239 offers another example of the composer's mixing tonic and dominant harmonies. As expected, Köhler and Bülow change the pedaling so that each harmony is clear. Martienssen and Casella, heretofore having often honored Beethoven's pedaling, also opt for clarity here. Taylor suggests in a note that these measures may need "modification" with regard to pedaling.

(h) Beethoven's long pedal marking sustaining dominant harmony from measure 295 to beat 2 of measure 312 is acceptable to all but two of the referenced editors. The A-flat and G octaves in the LH in measure 305–308 bother Casella and Taylor, who suggest a modification because of the sonority of today's piano. Tovey, on the other hand, encourages the performer to let the A-flat "growl mysteriously" against the G.

(i) From measures 314–327, the first edition fails to reproduce several of the sforzandi and dynamic marks evident in the autograph. This text shows the autograph version. Of special note are the parallel dynamic patterns of measures 321–323 and 325–327, wherein measures 321 and 325 start fortissimo, leading to a piano in measures 323 and 327. A decrescendo mark is found in measure 322, but is missing from 326. The composer's dynamic scheme seems clear in the autograph, but of the referenced editors only Arrau, Hauschild, Taylor, and Wallner take note of it. The remaining editors apply a pianissimo at measure 321.

attacca subito il Prestissimo

ⓙ The fingering in measures 465 and 467 appears in both the autograph and the first edition. It is generally agreed that the fingering indicates octave glissandi, a feat made easier on Beethoven's piano by its light action and more shallow key dip. Glissandi are still possible on modern day instruments for performers with sizeable hands. Wrist octaves are not possible at tempo, and none of the editors suggests slowing to accommodate them. D'Albert, Bülow, Casella, Martienssen, Schenker, and Schnabel each offer their arrangement for splitting the octaves between the hands. Splitting is fairly easy to achieve in measures 465–466 and 469–470 leaving out a note or two where the LH must execute large skips:

Measures 467–468 and 471–472 are more problematic because of the whole and half notes in the RH. Bülow, Casella, Martienssen, and Schenker resort to single notes in the LH (using lower octave notes). Schnabel splits the octaves between two hands indicating pedaling to sustain the RH chords, resulting in considerable blurring. D'Albert suggests an arrangement that this editor finds impractical at tempo:

ⓚ All editors agree that this trill should begin on the main note.

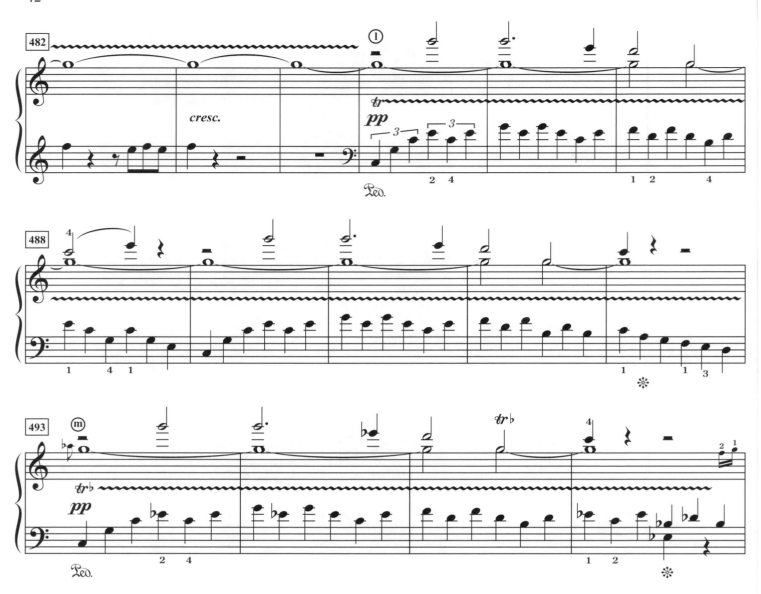

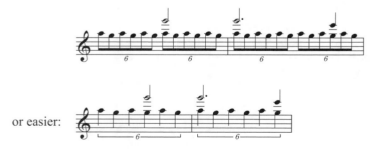

or easier:

① Beethoven's guidance for this passage was discussed in footnote ⓓ. Since the composer wrote his realizations in the context of this passage, his examples are reproduced here:

The composer's fragments, however, do not show how to proceed when the trill changes pitch or when after-notes (*nachschlag*) are involved. Several of the referenced editors attempt to clarify these issues by providing more nearly complete realizations of measures 485–507.

Bülow uses the "false trill" in eighth notes throughout maintaining upper accessories (see footnote ⓓ). Schenker and Schnabel keep the trill unbroken with the same approach, Schenker adding extra notes to accommodate *nachschlag* and Schnabel simply not including them. Schnabel suggests the possibility of using normal sixteenth notes (not sextuplets), a rhythmic arrangement this editor finds useful at tempo, notwithstanding the polyrhythm that develops (three against four) with the LH.

ⓜ In measure 493, the interval between A-flat and the G a major seventh above it results in a difficult stretch. This editor suggests playing the A-flat grace before the beat, thus shifting the trill to the main note at this point. This arrangement works well to accommodate the *nachschlag* at the end of measure 496, the octave in measure 497, the unison in measure 499, as well as the *nachschlag* in measure 500 (if they are used). In measure 501, the downbeat falls on the main notes and the D-flat grace note is before beat 2. Casella, incidentally, suggests much of this arrangement in a footnote.

(n) Neither the autograph nor the first edition show after-notes (*nachschlag*) here. D'Albert, Arrau, Bülow, Casella, Köhler, and Schnabel use them, however.

(o) Whatever adjustments may have been made in the preceding measures, editors advise that the grace notes in measures 507 and 511 should be on the beat and strong. This editor agrees.

(p) D'Albert, Bülow, Casella, Schenker, Schnabel, and Tovey offer one or both of the following facilitations:

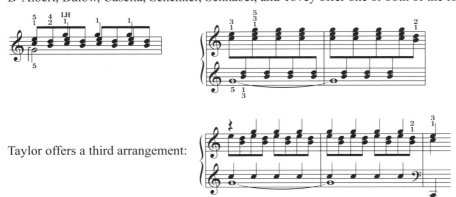

Taylor offers a third arrangement:

⒬ Neither the autograph nor the first edition close this pedal indication.